"That castle looks nice," said Mr Stein.

"Oh, you won't like that," replied Mr Flannel with a shudder. "No-one likes that."

"We will see it now," decided Mrs Stein.

Mr and Mrs Stein peered through the rusty gates at the old castle.
Mr Flannel had a nasty feeling that they were being watched.

"It does need a spot of paint to cheer it up," he stuttered.
"Oh no, it's fine," replied Mrs Stein. "Let's look inside."

"What a magnificent hall," commented Mr Stein with a flourish. "And it's fully fitted with wall to wall cobwebs — er, carpets," added his wife cheerfully.

But Mr Flannel wasn't listening. He had seen something hiding in the corner — something **very** strange indeed!

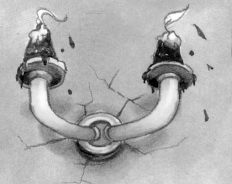

Next, they went to look upstairs. "The bedroom is a little ... breezy," said Mr Flannel, trying not to shudder as he looked out of the window.

"But a new pair of curtains will make all the difference," added Mrs Stein. And all her husband could say was "Lovely view!"

Mr Flannel was beginning to think that the Steins were a little odd.

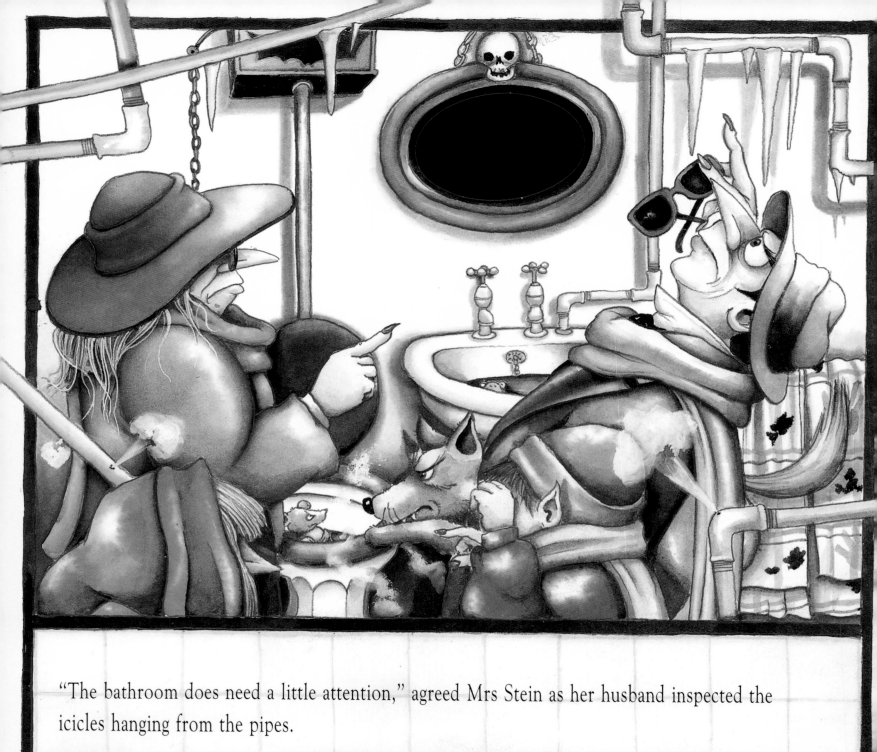

"The bathroom does need a little attention," agreed Mrs Stein as her husband inspected the icicles hanging from the pipes.

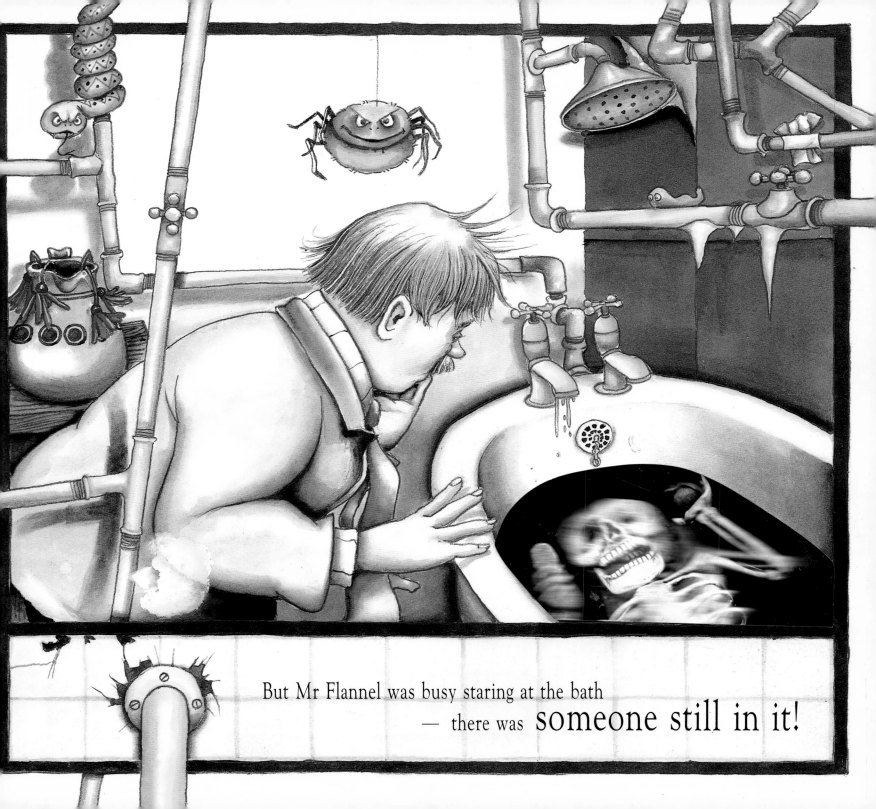

But Mr Flannel was busy staring at the bath
— there was someone still in it!

Mr Flannel led the way down the steep slippery steps to the cellar. "The cellar does have a small damp problem," he said, sneezing loudly as they gazed at the murky depths below.

Danny's eyes nearly popped out of his head! Something down there was moving. Something very odd indeed!